chain hearings aaron fogel

published by **inwood press** new york

distributed by **horizon press**

Some of these poems have previously appeared in
First Issue, *Boadway Boogie*, *Columbia Review*,
The Little Magazine, and *Sun*.

This publication is in part made possible with support
from the National Endowment for the Arts and from
the Coordinating Council of Literary Magazines.

Cover design: Riva Danzig

Printed in the United States

Library of Congress Catalog Card Number 75-13955
ISBN 0-8180-1530-6

for Barbara

Contents

I.

Chain Hearings

She was taken a second time for questioning. And so it went all night—after an hour or two she came back for ten minutes to the cell, didn't say anything, threw herself onto the plank-bed, and slept. But they always came to force her out of sleep again.
This is a favorite method, so-called chain-hearings.

—Margaret Buber-Neumann

1.
I kept losing the meaning of the word people
And so tired I couldn't go on with my business, caged the store.
Five-limbed and starry, the head in flight,
I went into isolate panics of vanishing.
The probe-light was on. A soldier led us
Through the corridor. Everything was dead and tiled.

Light was off. Lights were on the road.
Rain made flat circles on the windshield, driven
I stamped to the earth in a controlled tantrum
Of one foot. We were faster.

A beautiful voice said,
You don't have to give up everything for a sense
Of twining limbs. The false note is urgency,
Repairs needed by the mechanic not the jeep
To pay his bills.

                    Small boned and spellbound
Women and wounded elves find their safety
Where the shade drinks, and play in earth-hid water.
They don't want to know anything. Do you see this fist?

Anger can't find its way across its own imagery.
Where were the blisters blustering in heaven? the white cranes?
Closed the main door to the bank,
A revolver, the line going in through a regular pull door,
Twenty square feet of tile covered with blood
Were restored to their sheen in as many minutes
By janitors throwing sawdust. The teller said,
Refused him a loan and he shot himself, with a grin.
We do all of it too fast.

2.

For a few lines of beauty
hammering them out of white stone with swirls
the ocean interrogates the sand

and we come back to the cell swallowing sand
and back to the shore and to friends

The curved lines, where the waves flatten, meet
Rain makes flat circles on the windshield driven
are chain hearings, chain interrogations
to take false admissions of impossible crimes

impossible because
the state commits all that exist

3.

The road often looked as stupid as myself.
I was often half asleep as I went on.
I hallucinated while I drove and heard
The words and now shoot and now shoot.

She looked out the window
At a small airfield behind the highway.
"I clogged the drain at four in the morning.
I didn't want to make noise at that hour."

The hard lights and discussion went on
And they made her talk about good times,
When knights ate round a flat table,
Toasted each other, and praised praise.

They slowly exorcised everything human,
Imagining that the circus of their class
Was a pilgrimage.
Parents, deluged harps, floated
Because of their heavy frames.

4.
What do they mean about civilization
That if we protect it it will protect us?
All day I couldn't stand the truck's
Preaching and its de facto right of way.

An afternoon of dozing and lying together
Dreambutlered by a reappearing doe,
Her eyes like yours: large, they looked out
From Sumer and wire, enormously beautiful.

Historical conditions, those coins, flat circles
The doe leaps, the leaves act brilliantly
While the tree drinks and the truth lasts
While roots writhe in a cool dark place,

But coming up in lightning are destroyed
And the tree is prone but still half living.
We lie down but remain horizon divided.
Your waist is beautiful not dividing you.

Permitting ten minutes sleep, a stringed wood
On which each note can be played once
The music of breaking, the string split
So that growth is a tragic process.

5.
Sea's top frisks and the police.
Five of them beat someone on ninety-ninth.
Stripes of the flags dissolve into streaks.

Turning, the pages swallow, dry and nervous.
What we're afraid of is the world's order
Which will lead us where: to flat statements

With question marks, because the answerer's afraid,
And questioning structures
Without the raised voice that would make them so.

6.

The description of one case isn't salvation
But it's possible to bring them together, linking people
Who can't see the connections of suffering
And are cut off from everything but music.

Maybe the rubato of history expresses nothing
But those connections. Leivick in solitary
Thought his eyes would adjust to complete darkness
Until they didn't. He said rescuing angels come too late.

I'd give anything to protect my sister
Who cried in the foyer when she was seven.
I'd say words like this: have you been derided?
Felt everyone's rage? Picture springtails

Jumping off little indentations for tears
On a lake. She protects herself. That time has passed.
There never was a messiah without plague.
And there's an image answering that comfort

In every room, coke spilled on the floor,
A flat marsh, with no depth, and bubbles
That don't stop though they rise from nowhere.
They're cut off from everything but music.

7.
I thought my eyes would get used
to the complete darkness.
I walked up and down the cell

but had a sensation of speed.
Once when I was eight I fainted
though I was only bringing our cow

slowly at dawn to the market.
I felt as if I'd been running.
Now I tried to soothe myself

with boyhood memories
but couldn't arrange them.

Why because there was no clock
did I lose that sequence?
Why was darkness a disorder?

I don't like obscurity and grubbiness
but for most prisoners there's
a single weapon against the setting:

the tongue.
They curse the world, the sabbath,
the seasons of the year.

(After H. Leivick)

8.
Joke plans caused suicide
when she'd died
roots roamed on rocks
and nothing took.

The worm's a little mobile root
the grass his ideal statue.
sometimes it burns badly like tears
crying is best at the center.

Political idiots run the show and act
while looking at a stationary artifact
we can forget the speed, almost
imaginary, of bullets.

It's good we're out of weapons,
the task's harder.
it's easier to unleech a junta
than to take hands away from a sobbing face.

9.
Backwards to go is my dream
as light makes possible
when the badger and groundhog
return from spring.

Fire returning into hands,
leaves rising
to touch the tree
and the sun rising from darkness.

The horse absorbs his snort, pyramids play
and stand on their points
only Akhenaton wails
at the terrible sun come back from evening

And devils with their
enormous feet, modest torsos
and infinitesimal pointed heads
need no roots to stand

Therefore they talk
in the imperative past
Each of you must have done so
why else would you be here?

At this cemetery we're waiting
the priest
moves away from the stones
that await their bellying mound

When the carver achieves
the real life of the wood.

10.

Semitic core, belief in enemies
Round the table and under it,
Illumined by an eight-day lamp.
How can we light all-saints-day grins
Agree to be cheerful, and smile
With a false inner fire?
So not averting, a mind keeps
Tired eyes, dark circles, open
On the unexecuted drawing,
A thick black bloodstroked canvas.

It's forbidden to make images.
Staying with lyrics
And warm notes instead,
There are trumpets and words.
Sandstone goddess
Can be carved with carbide
But once they cut marble
With soft iron, repeatedly sharpening.

And if it's forbidden to make images
Is it also to imagine in words
Or in glistening, critical shouts,
Carving with those, and showing
Clouds in oil, the hiding faces?
But when I was allowed to paint
It was completely black canvases

To rest from the war of images,
Because the joined dolls and collage
Were nothing, magic, and power.

11.
The violence that deprived us of love
when we could still take dandelions and look
that made life passageways in the dark
through time, without doors, that jumped
our flesh from us till we had to learn it
by breathing under the care of thought

12.
October a dawn raid
the police import
a bunch of extra quiet
individuals to the hall
for questioning,
whose lives are minimal,
who seem to be
living in dreams
or are wandering the streets.
It's thought that
they know something
valuable, that
they might be keeping
a missing element
to themselves
and can make the descent
of greyness here stop
by telling their thoughts.
So we force them
to engage in dialogue
and they tell us nothing
worthwhile, though we beat them
and set them
through sleeplessness
we learn nothing again.

13.

In order to speak they arrange themselves. Chairs, vases,
    · badges, hats, straws.
Corpses in the reeds outside look at the sky, their hands under
    their heads for pillows.
Their faces are drawn in the water like oil with the sky giving it
    its colors.
Inside at night, hugging their pillows, the little rest adjustments,
    they dream that the corpses outside dream.
In the morning they wake up and find the daily arrangement or
    politics of the day that makes it possible to talk.
One has his belly on the floor, one hangs from the ceiling and
    welcomes jeers,
One takes up a meditative posture, one tries to become a
    twisting branch,
One teaches, one scratches his head, one puts science in song,
One sits in the doorway pulling hairs from his head and
    considering the little translucent wads on the ends,
One analyzes the five hundred and thirty two types of meetings
    and names them,
One pulls up grass and munches the white roots, one makes sly
    jokes, one has meetings in an old laundry,
One wears a green hat, one lies down, one hovers . . .

14.

A man carries a light, an unbearable brilliance, between rows of warriors. It frightens them and keeps them in line. Across the field the others are also preparing. On both sides, women cut out sheets and paint flags, working at wooden tables. They feel somehow that the battle will be more boring and lasting than the work.

To his surprise the man who carries is sent back to a place in the rows when he's finished the demonstration. He stands and meditates and a god comes to him. He begins to see, implied in the rows and colors, a carousing that gets its force from something that doesn't happen, and he doubts whether the carousing is only inside himself, or the true product of the arrangement of forms.

He also sees two women's faces, one expressing only pertinence, so that it's hard to meet her eyes, and the other impertinent, dazed and expressing nothing but a little beauty.

He begins to be afraid that all the rows are one lost being: if I withdrew I would only be a bastard or the familiar child staying out and obscuring the half-light with resistance.

After his death we sometimes discover that the enemy had fewer weapons than he pretended and we might have made him surrender without killing. But the spaces in our perception create wars, though the plea underneath the rows and costumes is "carouse." It's strange the way we let dazed impertinence wander around in this, singing and painting. We want her to do these things to leave us quiet and sadly obliged to her, leaving us doubtful about the beautiful forms we've used.

15.
(for erasers and jumpers)

She begs to erase the board
A privilege and gift
To turn her back on the class,
Ten seconds on each word.

The teacher doesn't see her.
She rubs at the dark slate.
A boy jumps out of his seat
And rackets with the chair.

The teacher whispers that
"He's a character,"
"Mother this, father that."
Finally slander

Aloud to the others reporting
His low reading score.
She says, "borderline."
He says, "I don't care."

She is still erasing,
Synchronized, unsynchronized
With the yells
She isn't facing.

A privilege and gift
To erase your blackboard—
More than thirteen ways
To look at it.

16.
Time disoriented
travel as despair
from place to place
no staying intimacy
or physical touch
in the "noosphere."

Dialogues are closer.
I want to hear
your thoughts:
the grasses throw
shadows on the ground
that are almost rooted
where the living is,
the flesh of earth
the hair of holding on.

But that talk is still not enough.
From the false axiom
there are no others
only things to arrange,
from licking the outside
of the bowl, self envy,
alone, envying ourselves,
to the crossing of awareness
holding on to the earth
by circling,
go out, and play.

17.
Not correctness or all the thoughts
I had could have changed the deadness
But your breath near mine made pints wake

And all the little qualities sang,
Each color, and each darkness, shadows,
The small lines, the shape of a leaf
And even its reason, no need to go on
Listing with words what the eyes see

The pain not gone but no longer magical
They take any anodyne for any fear
And go to rest, an entire generation
Dreaming of an even more crowded paradise
O exalted, exalted, small cries come down to us

18.

Life makes silence of the cold elements, stones, waters,
Imagining its own rest in them.
I turn away from my own voice,
Which is not something after all to look for
But yours, and the strength to hear it.

Not my own voice that delights me
After all this talking to myself
Wandering through the streets arguing
With someone as if I believed in prayer

The two extremes of loving, mystical, multiplied
In front of mirrors, and human
Naked in the woods, night dark leaves

19.
Bugs cluster on the timothy and fall off
Still together on the ground.

A world of little wars. Everyone
Looks up into proud noses for a while,
Then raises his own with contempt for what he saw.

The leaf has already fallen, but
Caught on a branch, seems to be attached.

A Brooklyner calls the sound
Of the ambulance a "sigh-ring."

That squirrel touching his heart is no
Opera singer, his paw is cold.

A cool green leaf is still cool green
After a cool green frog jumps off it.

20.

Where the light falls is its rind,
Summer fruits, or wildflowers in groups,
A merry company on a terrace
With sunlight, chairs, and beer flesh.

But here the city burns with it,
Sulfur protection, a night yellow
To stop theft in two dimensional light,
A medieval halo a flattening paint.

To draw the faces like water
Towards me with my hands to my face,
A morning dew, the light in the eyes
Washing and uncovering transparence.

The faces of squinting evergreen.
And end flat talk about auras when
Because of the camera no one shows
Us any more, the textures lost

In a shiny or scumbled print,
And pity, a figure in the doorway
His eyes smaller than the grating near him
Gazes at his own torn out hairs,

His drawn face a failed roundness.
To erase these dirty rings of Saturn,
And draw the faces and light undiscovered
By science, a corruptible angel

Running and running and hating the image
And flattening voices also,
Not showing, or unable to show
How the questions are being asked

With so much authority to get
Answered, in the enforced dialogue
That the questioner doesn't raise his voice
At the end, and the answerer can't.

II.

Landscape Without Earth

No, no stars visible in the sky
but all those soft lights across the river
as if the earth finally agreed to stop binding us
and come close with stars—

once you saw me almost disappear
now we can see the earth almost
disappear for the same reason

Red Clouds

Red clouds at night over the city
laughing at marble and pick-ups.
The paradox of society
the best company's a stranger.
Your truest friends
don't yet define you.
She smiles, I feel washed
of the entire past and hopeful.
We met and stayed
undefined, except by presence
the mystery of the first night
your whiteness in the darkness.

Poem

their fear of continuity
as the spokes of the sun
merge, their fear of
continuity as the gold sun
merges onto a million leaf
plates, their fear of
continuity which
braces one life onto a day
as a bronze sun is braced
as an ornament on a wall,
the continuity of fear
their parental fear of
continuity their fear
of their children their
love of their grandchildren

Pine Needles

Pine needles, sharp
Make soft shadows
Clusters with assertions
The shadow of a pine
A mass with rough edges
Be starfish and grow back
Vaguer and wilder edged
Than coins and violence
Wind moves the shadows

Moths

It was in Connecticut
In the beginning of the night
We were standing on a bridge
With a million moths

And looking down into the water
Of the Housatonic
When we saw a man coming toward us
Rugged and broadshouldered

Sending out attack rhythms
And when he passed us
It turned out to be a woman
Dressed in an army jacket

Who asked about the police siren
And the cars that just went by
And then went into a long
Tirade about the local police

They had arrested her son
For no reason
And insulted his grandma
An old woman

We were looking at the water
We took some cigarettes
She went on talking
About the mad police

We edged to our car
While she was still talking
Not letting us go
Asking for agreement

The bridge was full of moths
More than I've ever seen
They avoided the headlights
When we drove by again

Spider Monkeys Whirling

"Is whispering nothing?" (Leontes)

Whistling's ended war and sparrows fencing fields
speak peace that passes through and triumphs
and commands wrestling doves "make your eyes tangent now"
so that small black circles collide to touch
and look in at each other.

The spider monkeys, falling leaves,
can almost make their prison trees.

One more swing of emaciated tree flight and
the fences are gone, brown meager wanderers.
They look up with close eyes, the meaningful beggars.
The eyes of the wind.

"To be at home in the trees
without a stake in anything but displacing
lots of air was beauty.

                    "But here are bare bars
and it's getting cold, and dark, the public's coats
weigh them down. Autumn. We'd go away. Small birds
light off terror leaving a branch they bend
or sit clown warriors in the moonlight.
Is whistling nothing? Leg-bands would come off, thatch
be loosed, the sky be shown on time into the house
and meanings never thought out castle in wind's leaf."

Torpor

We're made for torpor
like memories or owls
Her round face changes
when she lies down

It's shameful to work
obediently with bags
that become opaque
when the food in them leaks

Don't thrash to bring
everything to completion
facing facts like idiots
the next morning in bandages

You whisper the news
to me in the hall
Why talk so low
about your raise?

Plaster

Plaster is the symbol
used to be dust
white, warming up
while it sets
cold when finally set.

Plaster is the symbol
composing walls
out of slop
or adapting itself
to duplicate.

Plaster is the symbol
impermanent and cheap
a century
pure and soft
before drowning.

Plaster is the symbol
hiding from water
even after immersion
in clumps and clusters
in unbaptized groups.

A Basin

A basin chipped, chipped
    will rust and carry water
        and light
in the public school
    a beaten woman yells
        at her pupils
and the eye is sad
    and the children dance
        and are sad anyway

Children always laugh
    and cooperate it isn't
        your personality
it's their life
    so take care what plastic
        animals you make
them worship

Poem

Mental pain is God, steering us
as gently as possible toward
another conclusion than we are fixed on—
breakdowns as common as pigeons
in this city and each one thinks his own
is special, until he is over it,
and it ends when it no longer seems special—

delicate as a wart the mistake,
so proud so well kept up.
the river has some campers on it
looking warlike, steered by the bearish fathers
whose salvation, or complete
lack of it both are suggested
by their acceptance of violence

in which way Calvin is still with us
you can't figure, or tell
what people mean by their convictions,
or gestures, you can only smell something,
which the silvered violence of the sky
tells us is the original perception,
the shudder

Summer

The city's a ladybug back, a sullen design
Warning bits of unrelated color
Advertisements, red herring omens, multiply.
Something opposite to sunlight
Crosses their bodies, an off-me loneliness.

Soft white sand, bright plaster, beach dust,
Near water but unsoftened, seeds of glass,
Says lie down here, warm yourselves.
Splinter legged big idiotic birds
On the shore seem lonely to them, not mating.

Autumn behind glass, a green gold ibis,
Thoth in a museum, with carved claws,
A scythe beak, cruel obedience, glares.
He can't let the cruelty in his eyes leak.
He could become urine from all that staring

And swell to a sickly bladder, green and gold,
But doesn't. He has enough to eat, tears
On the beak, pearls, and an empty Easter egg,
Wisdom, sand into glass, not muddy shores.
We lie down as we are, stupid and warm.

Storms

Lambs run to get the newspapers off their backs
Then flowers
Surround the papers and eat them up
The fields stay clear
Snap your dragon hands
I ask my friends to stop giving me advice
Because they'll be right
They push the storms back with their palms
And dry up the earth

I thought you were dying all that time you were living
Snap your dragon hands to become one with the hills
Bulbs that are too bright for looking at and too dark for seeing
The rooms are square in the storm
And have a different order
From brushed hair
They don't cause equal distribution but clusters
Not as beautiful as sound clusters in music or other clusters
But people in groups faced inward

When storms brush the earth let's grab each other
Exactly at the same time
Bounce around the room beauty and bitterness mixed
Children prying beauty from the table top
We fly up not regretting and land as whole as always
The storms that brush the earth
Are on top and skim the shining earth
Who was polished by a hand that never touched her

Her shining and her untouchability are the same
And keep us all safe no
When the storms brush the earth
What shows itself on what is
Is love bouncing off us like light
"If we've gone away
How do we know we can come back"
A horse stops in the air
And becomes one of a thousand trapped clouds
The sun comes out and makes us sneeze
The ground sneezes
One of the ways sun gets you moving

Werad Deru

At all costs find strength for your own voice
which catches at first, nail on the string
but twangs louder at the passage,
breaks brooms, dries the cured wood,
and the handle hay, splits the apple, and makes merry.

What's our marriage?
October air only,
ghosting pillow, soften the head
evergreen stinging, a murmur
white raging at color?
is it only white as darkness? mist?

                              In reconstructed Indo-European
                              werad is the root for word and root
                              deru the root for tree and truth,
                              they are the same word mirrored
                              in consonants, werad, deru
                              root and tree.
                              They felt the shape of the word
                              and were aware that a tree grew into the
                                                  ground
                              and another life on the other side

And you get through the mist
the one I want to sing to
so that my head holds up
not with the pride of hurt but gladly

Runaways

Their parents ran away from home
and not meaning to, deprived them of the joy of running for
    themselves.

they would be imitators, and stayed
in a palace that was decaying fast,

a few days of food in the fridge,
dust, dying ivies,
a lot of drugs in the sink cabinet
and the quickly left, crumpled bedroom the horror

with some dresses only and some suits gone
soft pillows left, the other car
to ride around in and crash up,
a short thrill.

It is the parents that run most often not the kids
the cop said but not in these neighborhoods usually. To leave
an ambiguous mansion filled with conveniences
and a sprinkler to dance in, not the city heavy hydrant

or else why did they run?
and a lot to take care of and to lose.
Where did the parents go and what
should they do now, watch shadows

on tv and lie in beach chairs
during the day and wait
likewise for the promiscuous water the hatred
to flood up and rush them out of the house?

The Cats

She thought she was ugly but slept with men she thought were
    beautiful
Didn't she know how beautiful she was how ugly I was
Her eyes overthrew governments inside me
She was so ugly I would've fallen off cliffs to keep her with me
And didn't have to she thought she was crooked
And hated mirrors once in a while glanced there
I used to throw her in front of the mirror
Like a cat to see if there'd be a reaction

Sitting in a purple chair she looked sadly around the room
Raised a corner of her mouth not annoyed but disappointed in
    herself
At night she turned terrifying couldn't see her long soft hair
Any more than her future she took eight steps with each step
I backed her to the wall to touch her
Time refused to reveal itself so she agreed she ran away
She tore a sheet she lounged in the bath she was happy

Furious I threw a dictionary at her and she caught it
Threw it back and knocked me unconscious

I lay on the varnished floor in darkness or blankness
She tells me her hands lifted my embellished head
And honeyed my eyes I don't believe it
When I came to she was sleeping next to me
We were in the arena of our room
The cats tore at the door wanting to get in
Not to see us but to explore
We let them in and they agonized over the quilt
We were better than them our nails were longer
We'd been asleep for days
They leaped to the ledge and looked out

The River on the Boat

1.

       Clays. In one area trees.
It's dawn, she fingers her hair and is too white.
Red lap, sound of the river on the boat
The gods' answers revolve too fast
To see the spokes, that shine
Retroactively, and seem like
Going backward.

       Red dawn. Clay man. Terra cotta. Come down.
We don't dissolve playing in the water
Meteors and water dissolve
Shrieks, laughing and thigh-slapping in the boat
Green hills that rise and fall. A herd.
Grazing is ripping.

       Nothing stays but forces,
Circles on the water,
The lap clapping, the boat, being born
And meeting its own rings,
Applause in one creature heard by another,
All other applause the sound of falling cities

2.

       "I'm Ethel from downstairs I'm the switchboard
Operator, I know all the names but I don't
Know all the faces." Read the laws and remain
Level, like lakes that read the laws
And hold boats obediently.

Around them are trees. Then
Rails, and wire, and behind that

Rama and slate. Skirts, Stars,
Groundless except for the paper ones
Given as rewards, the cloth ones sewn.

All's gone. Sheer sympathy.
Broken-hearted gamblers, thrown in a pit,
Chosed a long time ago for something,
Brooks or the secret grain or poppies,
Yesterday we took the subway. God's eyes
Slam shut on the browsers, and the gold
Cross garnishee sleeps off a day's work.

3.
The boat was a bad image, we left it
It meant wooden sides and floating
Without contacting water
So that making discoveries in it was a drunk
A field of names.

Red dawn. Clay man. Terra cotta. Come down.
The warm blooded sea animals are ugly, and smile.
They embarrass and ring you with a flat heat,
Finding them. The fisherman throws them back.
The leaves embrace
When they think no one's watching. The stars
Touch when the telescopes are off.

Gods pine by the icy airfield.
Ceramics drift, a kind of shellfish
In the ocean. We dive and return.
The people, a walking water,
What doesn't become false when it's spoken.

The Higher Steps *(after Friedrich Klopstock)*

I'm often there in dreams, where there is no more dreaming.
Though close to God I still hurry
in fields my eyes haven't seen
or my mind made.

Round me more grace than in forests and streams
on earth. Fire springs up
from mountains, but is also the mild warmth
of dawn gushed in the valley.

Clouds change when I come near them, and I see the living
    nature
of different forms. Each form
often becomes another. They seem to outdo themselves
in beauty when they change.

These immortal bodies are like stilling fragrances
they send holy glimmers, and like the moment, when
truth or an invention found,
you enjoy happiness:

When they become new forms they turn to look at the fields.
Then they sink back
into the refreshing fire
that pours from the mountain head.

Do the immortals speak through changing images?
These do:
with what feeling
they speak about God.

Happiness is often climbing
upward, to become happier.
I followed each one who spoke with me,
and waking, I saw the evening star.

III.

Minimal Lives

1.

Trades rhetoric, long lines to the teller
Shamming love for the world, so much love.
This is the age when we get professional.
He paints his fingernails, says "my hands are dirty"
And, "if I find myself thinking too much I know
I'm in bad shape." Sense and sensuality burnt off
By a fear of thinking, and here and there
From odds and ends to extract an illusion of triumph.
Success has its beauties, the world its ugliness
So success builds itself out of pretended love
For the world, what we see, where we live.
And to have more intellect than personality
Is nothing but the original sin against glamor.

2.

The struggle within the ivied class
the son of a judge grows up to be
shapeless and depressed, a man on a bench,
the war businessman's son becomes
an arts organizer, the advertiser's
a publicist for teaching methods,
the farming of the same cultural earth,
our fathers vergers and die-makers
we're teachers and disc-jockeys,
the static throat, factory scrapings,
radio music, the voice choked by rage
into joking, and laughing in, not out,
with a strange hoarseness, unable even
to give the air of its laugh away,

and the real inheritance
is not psychological but jobs,
and the son of the businessman speaks
about knowing poets the way his father
and mother speak about having money.

3.
The son of a father who spoke in putdowns
and parries only becomes a young poet who
admires Berryman or Creeley, the nearness of
the nastiness of speech, and he's faced with
mutual praisers, the way of levelling
without really levelling, the holding together
of a professed fabric ignorant of the body's
reasons not to be part of the fabric to be
slips cut off from the current tight-erotic fashion.

4.
"Whites tend to think
that it's below their dignity
to show just suffering"
"But the time to abandon
the literature of misery
hasn't yet arrived"

The Letter Reader

They did not seem to me like friends
but like dead birds
with an ideology of closeness
pecking stones on the ground
into forms like themselves.

Talking about sex, talking about triumphs,
their own personal growth,
the dead birds were in my room
asking me why I didn't talk
more about sex, more about energy.

Their stones were all around them
in the room. Months later
they separated and he stayed
while I was away on vacation, in my room
and he read the love letters

Written to me, without asking me,
because he was curious,
because he always needed to know more
about the words for the things,
always trying to find out.

Then his wife, to tell him
what she couldn't tell him
left her diaries open on the bed
when he visited, so that he saw
the notes about her other affairs.

I see him on the bed, hunched
like a dead bird on the road,
reading, always finding out
the thing he cannot know, the thing he must know
the dead birds talking about love.

And The Wine Is Red
With The Shame Of Hustling

passive suffering continues
it did not end
with the end of the romantic era
and revolutionary activity
and the ideology of
undefined energy-levels
don't remove its light.

there are green tragedies
the bud scolded
back into death by winter—
you were born too soon—
and the misery of vegetation
on a dying earth
is passive.

action is too large a thing
to fight chemicals—
a lively person can burst
chains, but punching
won't remove chemicals
from the blood
in the fist.

and sometimes you vomit
and then lie still
to counter a poison.
so with the earth
and only the market-
place is now selling
''energy'' and ''action''

& those who, young
and ambitious, cite
Reich or Blake,
who were earlier than
we are, to justify
the ways of god
for the man
are destroying energy
which must have
form in time.

the wheel is constantly
turning, constantly eroding,
leaving words depleted
and selfish, like heroes
after they've served
their historic purpose
slaughtering herds of sheep,
dreaming they are still
useful.

the high vowels break the armor
and seem less beautiful later
after they've done their work
for you, and become coarse:
they are Los's
hammer and Reich's pounding,
but now we can pay
the debt of song to ourselves.

Twilight Away From Home

1.
Pre-named the horse is born.
why do I hear the sound of a horn?
Cooperate until there's no more sound
except another gallop and sometimes
flood from the sky.
Nor browbeat time
till her hands cover her face
or life, random and set like marble.

2.
Nomadic past travestied by deportation,
not wanderers or explorers, travel their doom,
the forced voyagers with a thin image of survival

resigned to motion, a political thing,
a grief that jumps on straight tracks

freight, and the untrained gardener
had let too many grow
past borders he could control

so that though kidnapped tars had done
past work also, it didn't matter
this century's forced mass movements

weren't old or new or transient
—mistakes.

Entrenched laborers like pills
take a while then work,
the understood sun our breakwater.

3.
The hard-backed pigeon
and the blank-backed emblem
want square cups of grain
and will flatten ladders.
What don't they knock down
to get their arrangement?
Their hypochondria makes them
sodomize their heads to the earth
or walk, not fly.
They're the city's animals,
faces of sockets, two rectangle
non-eyes and a long non-mouth.
The sorcerer's veto killed them—
I'm not damaged I'm damage he said
and they didn't know what he meant
self-pity or threat but he forbade.
The antidote to rows
was sunlight odor and the soft shoulder
of an arm raised to point direction.
The hawk's eye smells lacquer
at the top of the mind
When did you lose your father?
I didn't lose him he died

They Grew Up Too Fast
for Jitu Borpujari

You stepped on a nest of snake eggs when you were a kid.
They were born suddenly, and you thought they were playing
when they fought with each other, until you saw that some
of them were dead. You said this stuck with you.

The hailstones in Assam come down as big as this, you
make a ring out of your thumb and forefinger. After a
storm we go out to look for, how would you translate it,
hail birds.

There are mild earthquakes and when the rumbling hits
we run outside. Everyone's screaming call to God, call
to God—hari bul, hari bul. You double over laughing,
"it may seem funny to you everyone going around crying
horrible, horrible." Hari means lord, bul means chant.

Jitu, I also had a sense of growing up too fast, but
in a different way. Mixing time with many. Jugglers,
tossing and catching torches, one always in the air, don't
show their skill but the scarcity of their hands.

Around Cambridge, icons in wee churches included a leering,
cross-eyed lion with his tongue out. Roundhead flower!
jet eyed proud shot through green and gold! yellow
puppet mortalized in stained glass!

In the porn shop take a look at how the human image is doing. The young girls shove their cunts forward with puzzled contemning faces in the expression that means "you know what this is I don't."

Though it's said in the Talmud that when all the possible combinations of letters and words are written the messiah will come, reduce it to the secular and say that when people start writing a lot of nonsense it's because there's no messiah and they're daring him to come.

To stand aside and watch her dance. The desire to reach her overtakes me with movement.

Images of Resting and Working at the Same Time

bicycle smoothly running by a wood
road fence unpainted made even softer by rain

carrying and being carried
near the red poppies and white birches

jogger near the broken benches in the park
slats painted each year and bolted

but a wood vandal comes
who wants more air in his bench

go on in the soft costume a pillow
a small rest-adjustment a sleeper fidgeting

run through the park sleeping
and twitching into physical perfection.

even happier at dawn
we hadn't slept happy for the rain

in the field the sheep were bleating
inside a newsprint surface of wool

only the restive spirit of the semi-domestic
in a minor field.

the green rode its hills we were chosen
animals and danced.

the matches burn softly
fire is a fine twill twined upward

it discards the coarser twill of the luminous
till there's nothing left of itself

a perfectionist dispersed
and leaving some worthless carbon.

but feet, great resters
khorusein, to be about to dance

and make impermanent blisters on the ground
the way the sun brings out orange rind

the thickness of world rebuff or intuition
skin thickness that can take the sun's touch

without burning up wanting in this life

immanent sun or reason streaming down
and making a soft clamor with the ground

Stinging the Bee

We have to knock down
The ladder that's already on the ground.

Our feet have buds
That have been used to hoist us onto branches.

We swing in the wind unconscious,
Absalom-by-the-toes looking earthward.

Our part in nature
Has been used to make us unaware.

We have to knock down the ladder
The ties the "fellers" have built,

Which are already horizontal,
Which no one has to knock down,

And use it for a fire,
A green fire, a burial.

We have to sting the bee
Flicking a finger on its nose,

So that it gets confused,
And buzzes without harm.

And place the fellers
On the ladders they built

That hide the earth in motion
Between manufacturing places.

Let them lie down on the ladder.
The ladder will divide their wealth.

They call discoverers of butterflies' groins
Geniuses, and insulate themselves not the wires.

They end up forced to paint their fingernails
To be able to claim that their hands are dirty.

When their bodies are stretched on the ladder
They'll return into as many fragments

As there are classes: the ladder
Is hierarchy, the bee is violence.

Unexpected Carriers of the Sun

There's no more room in the world for the world
has become a shell,
a place of hard waves that circle—
as if wise—the poor being beaten
screamed tonight, let me go, hoarsely
for fifteen minutes, till quieter
across the alley, so the police were called
and told, someone is being murdered, somewhere.

Then a soft flood rocked us to sleep bluish movies on tv
which end at 5:34 a.m., the moment of dawn
so that the pallor on the blank set is the same
brillance as the sky.

The sprigs are bright around the housing
the photographed twins, something gloomy in
                              organic identicals
a girl spreads her legs in the stairwell fifth floor
on jury duty the businessman frets talks about clones
explains, making duplicates of an organism
by grafting from one cell into life

and he's devising a method to turn sound into sight
and when we install his tv's in our heads
they'll take up less room than they do now
and then we'll see nothing, absolutely
reading the braille of our convolutions

put in general terms, unconscious pimping
selling green and fickle Ishtar for a tar and feather road hat

pagan treats. but
though there are no people they can turn

the clones are
turning on you

the dolphins' backs
appear here unexpected and sanctioned
by another god.

here are figures who don't turn
but dance,

here's turning in any direction
not just four,
the pine leaves' radial swim on the air.

the fir floats. wide and blurry.
seals and dolphins. noisemakers.

and here are people though there are no such things
turning on the streets.